Waylon!

One Awesome Thing

Waylon!
One Awesome Thing

SARA PENNYPACKER

PICTURES BY
Marla Frazee

SCHOLASTIC INC.

ISBN 978-1-338-21328-7

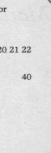

12 11 10 9 8 7 6 5 4 3 2   17 18 19 20 21 22

Printed in the U.S.A.   40

First Scholastic printing, September 2017

Waylon!

One Awesome Thing

1

Waylon craned his neck. "Moon at the nearest point in its orbit—check. Clouds—check. But Joe, I'm telling you—"

"Are you sure about the clouds?" Beside him, Joe squinted at the sky. "They look so fluffy."

"Oh, they have plenty of mass," Waylon assured him. "A medium-sized cumulus cloud weighs as much as eighty elephants. But remember, the effect will barely be—"

"Don't forget the Airbus A380. That plane is huge. There it is, on the horizon." Joe flattened

3

himself against the brick wall and chalked a mark at the top of his head.

Waylon sighed. Joe used to be the shortest kid in the class. He was pretty much normal-size now, thanks to a recent growth spurt, but he was still height-crazy. Last week Waylon had made the mistake of mentioning to him that Skylab astronauts had each grown two inches due to zero gravity. "That's it!" Joe had cried. "Gravity is what's keeping me down! You're science-y—do something!" He'd been pestering Waylon ever since.

"Remind me how this is going to work?" Joe asked now.

"Something really dense and really close, like the earth, has a lot of gravity," Waylon explained again. "But you could counteract it a little bit by stacking the moon, the clouds, and

4

the Airbus above you. But seriously, it probably won't be enough to notice."

"How much?"

"Maybe an angstrom, which is really small, Joe! It takes about twenty-five million angstroms to make an inch."

"I'll take it!" Joe said. He pressed his shoulders to the wall and grinned.

Actually, Waylon was kind of excited, too. He was buying a special journal this weekend. In it, he would record his life's work as a scientist. Lately he'd been concentrating on gravity, and he was expecting a big breakthrough soon. If today's experiment worked, *Counteracted gravity to help a friend get taller* would look great on the first page of his new journal. "Here comes that plane, Joe," he cried. "Get ready!"

Just then, Arlo Brody ran up. He head-butted Waylon on the shoulder—not hard, but still, Waylon went sprawling.

Arlo jerked his thumb, and Joe trotted off with a grateful look on his face, as though he'd been waiting all recess for someone to send him away, never mind the getting-taller nonsense.

Arlo Brody was like that—he only had to suggest something, and a person magically felt that it would be an incredible honor to do that exact thing. Waylon suspected the phenomenon was related to Arlo's hair, which stuck up like a crown. Arlo sure acted as if he was king of the whole school, and all the other kids acted like his subjects.

Waylon watched sadly as the clouds parted, and the Airbus zoomed away. It might be a long time before there was another perfect opportunity. But just then, Arlo smiled down at him, and Waylon felt as if he were basking in the warm glow of royal rays. His mouth automatically smiled back.

Arlo helped Waylon up. "I told you yester-day, you're on my team. You're supposed to spend recess with us. We have a name now. Shark-Punchers."

A bunch of boys had followed Arlo. They bared their shark teeth and head-butted each other.

"Shark-Punchers. That's our signature move," Arlo explained. "Get it?"

"Well, but . . . sharks can't punch." Waylon worried that might have sounded offensive, so he added a "Sorry."

Arlo threw a double punch at the air. "Sure they can. They have fins."

Waylon had no choice but to correct him. Science was science. "No. A shark's fins are hydrodynamic. They provide lift like plane wings. And they pivot to change the angle of attack. Also, sharks use them to signal other

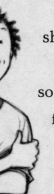

sharks. But they can't punch."

"Whatever," Arlo said with a grin so big that Waylon's own cheeks hurt from returning it. "Look, it took me a while to decide whether to put you on my team or not. The blurting-out thing? Like the mucus stuff on Monday? Remember?"

Waylon remembered. Mrs. Fernman had just pointed to New Zealand on the map. Waylon had shot out of his seat. "There are these amazing glowworm caves there, except they're not really glowworms, they're fungus gnat maggots, and they drool long glow-in-the-dark mucus strings to attract insects. It's so awesome!"

Everyone, except for Mrs. Fernman, had cracked up. This happened a lot when he shared something he'd learned on his favorite show, *Miracles of the Natural World*. He didn't understand the reaction—if someone had just told him something so interesting, he would be thanking that person, not laughing. But he had never minded it.

Until right now. *The "blurting-out thing"???*

"But even with the blurting-out thing," Arlo went on, "you're obviously a brain. I'm putting the brains and the jocks on my team."

Arlo beamed another shiny smile, and once more Waylon beamed it back.

Why had he done that? Waylon didn't want to be put on any team at all. He wished Arlo hadn't started the whole team thing in the first place. So why had his mouth just smiled back at Arlo?

Alien Hand Syndrome, he knew, was

a rare disorder where a person loses control over one of his or her hands. It was his absolute favorite of all the conditions listed in Chapter Five, "Bizarre but True," in *The Science of Being Human*. But he'd never heard of Alien Mouth Syndrome.

Waylon forced his lips into a non-smiling position. "Are those the only choices?" he asked. "Brains or jocks?"

"You could be both, like me, but otherwise, yeah, one or the other. Except for Willy." Arlo crooked a finger at the Shark-Punchers, and Willy trotted out.

Willy looked anxious. Of course, he had been looking anxious since Day One of fourth grade. This was because for the first time he wasn't in the same class as his twin sister, Lilly. For weeks now, he had been skittering around in a state of nervous panic.

"Willy's our artist," Arlo explained.

Waylon bit his lip to keep from saying *But Willy can only draw sharks. Clementine is the artist in our class,* because he knew what Arlo would say. Arlo had explained the rule yesterday: *Teams are boys only.*

"He's going to draw our logo. A shark, punching. Remember? All he has to learn to draw

is the punching part. Easy. Right, Willy?"

Arlo seemed proud of this idea, but Willy looked petrified. Arlo threw an arm around his shoulders. "Forget the fins. Just make the shark's head a fist. With teeth. Okay?"

Willy looked around desperately. Waylon could tell he expected Lilly to be right beside him, telling him what to do.

"Disambiguation, Willy. Phantom Limb Syndrome," Waylon explained in a soothing tone. "When an arm or a leg gets amputated, people still feel like it's there. You have Phantom Sister Syndrome."

Now Willy appeared even more terrified of Waylon than he was of Arlo. "My sister wasn't *amputated*!" he howled. "She's just in *Room 4C*!" He dove back into the bunch of Shark-Punchers.

Arlo shot his pack a grinning thumbs-up, which they all returned. He spun back to Waylon. "We can get started now. Everyone's on a team."

Waylon scanned the playground. The girls were sprinkled all around, playing or talking in little groups. But it was true that the fourth grade boys were divided. Half were clumped behind Arlo. The other half lined the fence, keeping a nervous eye on Arlo's clump. "What do we have to do?" Waylon asked.

"I told you yesterday. Stuff," Arlo answered. "Against the other team."

"Why?"

"Because they're against us."

"Why?"

15

"We're against them. Doing stuff. Come on, let's go. It's going to be cool."

Waylon considered the Shark-Punchers. Lots of his friends were there. Matt, whose mother worked at the aquarium. Matt let him explore behind the tanks with him whenever he wanted. Rasheed, who'd been building a duct-tape city with him since first grade. Zack, who was teaching him soccer.

Then he looked over at the other group. A lot of his friends were there, too. Charlie was the funniest kid in fourth grade. He and Waylon were working on a cartoon strip about astrophysics. Marco was studying to become a famous chef. He tried out new recipes on weekends and shared the leftovers with Waylon on Mondays. Next to Marco was Joe, who shared his dog, Buddy, with Waylon sometimes. Joe was so nice, he even let Waylon call Buddy

Galaxy, and Buddy was so nice, he answered to it.

Waylon didn't get it. Until last week, everybody in the class had been friends, or at least they hadn't been not-friends. Why had Arlo gone and messed that up?

Just then, the Recess-Is-Over bell rang.

Arlo charged off to herd the Shark-Punchers to the front of the line. The other team gathered at the back.

Waylon stood alone in the middle. He felt a terrible collapsing sensation in his chest, as if a black hole had just swallowed his heart.

2

Joe and Charlie came over while Waylon was waiting for the bus. "Sorry about recess," Waylon told Joe. "We can try again next full moon."

"That's okay," Joe said. "What did Arlo want? Did he finally put you on our team?"

"And did he give us a name yet?" asked Charlie. "Something great, like theirs—the Shark-Punchers?"

Waylon sighed. "That's not a great name. Sharks don't punch."

Joe shrugged. "Still great. So, what does Arlo call us?"

"He just calls you the other team."

Joe and Charlie both shrugged at that. "Okay. We'll be the Others. What should our signature move be?"

Charlie and Joe shrugged at each other again, and Waylon thought, *A shrug—that's your signature move.* He shrugged back.

"And a logo. We heard the Shark-Punchers are going to have a logo, so we need one, too," Charlie said. "You could draw it, Waylon. Make it science-y. I know—something science-y punching. How about a space monster?"

"Monsters are the opposite of science-y, Charlie. Extraterrestrials are science-y. Besides, Arlo's putting me on his team."

"No!" Joe looked as if he'd been punched,

20

and not by a shark. "You'd be against us. You can't be against us."

"But you're against them."

"Well, sure. They're against us!" Charlie and Joe: more shrugging.

"But Arlo's my friend. So are a lot of other kids on his side."

"But we're your friends, too." Joe got a crafty look in his eyes. "And so is Buddy. I mean Galaxy. You can't be on a team against Galaxy."

Galaxy! Waylon could picture him so clearly it hurt. Galaxy, looking up at him with eager brown eyes, one ear up and one down, a Frisbee in his mouth, and then . . . trotting away.

"I don't want there to be teams at all," Waylon muttered.

Just then, the first bus opened its doors, like a big shark mouth, and Waylon watched Joe and

Charlie run off together. When his bus came, he took a seat at the very back and pressed his face to the cool window.

Recently, a strange thing had been happening, and it was happening now. The strange thing was: he imagined how he appeared to others. As though he was outside his body, watching himself.

Not extraterrestrial others. Extraterrestrials watching wouldn't bother him at all. If they were looking down from their space pods,

Waylon felt sure they would *grok* him. *Grok* was a word he'd learned in a science fiction story. It meant to understand something so completely you practically merged with it.

No, it wasn't extraterrestrials he worried about, it was other human kids. And when Waylon imagined other human kids watching him, he imagined them laughing—not nice laughs, but mean smirks.

Why is that boy sitting alone at the back of the bus like a loser? those imaginary kids would ask each other now with big, mean smirks. *Arlo Brody, king of the school, wants him on his team— he should be happy. What's his problem, anyway?*

Seeing himself from the outside made Waylon feel dangerously sheer, as if he were a hologram instead of a solid boy.

Luckily, though, he had discovered that if he could find a perfectly quiet place—no easy feat in the middle of Boston, Massachusetts—he could hear himself living. From the inside. And hearing himself from the inside had the opposite effect from seeing himself from the outside. It made him feel solid again.

When the bus dropped him off, Waylon tore into his building and raced through the condo, slowing down only enough to yell "School was fine!" before his dad could come out of his writing studio and ask about it.

He skidded into his room, dug under his bed for the earmuffs his grandmother had sent him, then ran out again. He yanked open the heavy door to the fire stairwell and pounded down the steps.

And there, in the silence of the double-thick concrete stairwell, he crouched under the bottom flight of steps, clapped the earmuffs to his head, squeezed his eyes shut, and listened.

Not to the sounds of his heart beating and his blood pumping through his veins. Anybody could hear those sounds just by listening medium-hard.

He listened *underneath* those sounds. To the tiny music of life: the infinitesimal cracklings of bone growth, the little zaps of electricity charging his brain, and the hushed whooshes of oxygen exchanging with carbon dioxide in his lungs.

It is one thing to know you are alive on this earth, but it is quite another to actually hear the proof.

In the comfort of the living-Waylon sounds, he totally forgot about teams and whether anyone might be smirking at him.

But then he noticed something: every once in a while, the living-Waylon sounds disappeared.

He pressed his palms over the earmuffs and listened harder. Yes, microsecond silences, randomly occurring.

Waylon tugged his hair up. Even though he knew perfectly well that it didn't make any more room for his brain, doing this always made it *feel* easier to think.

And the answer came. It was obvious, but so amazing, it was hard to believe.

A shiver thrilled up his spine. He jumped to his feet and tore off the earmuffs. A scientific achievement this huge would make him famous the instant he announced it.

But before he could announce it, a scientific achievement this enormous needed a witness.

He ran back up to his condo and, inside, banged on the door that was painted black. "Neon, I need you! You have to come with me!"

Waylon's sister opened her door and slumped

against the doorway. She looked as if she'd been trying to scribble herself out. Black eyeliner, black lipstick, black nail polish. She studied him for a good long time.

"What," she demanded, flicking her fingers through the spikes of her scribbly black hair, "is the point?"

On the day she'd turned fourteen this past summer, Charlotte Brontë Zakowski had undergone a complete metamorphosis. Instead of spinning a chrysalis around her, she had walked into her bedroom and painted it black. When she'd emerged, she was wearing ripped black tights on her arms and legs, and over those, a variety of tattered black rags. She'd reminded Waylon of a bat who'd had a close call with a shredder. "My name is Neon now," she'd announced, then gone back into her cave and slammed the door.

Since then, Neon had been What-is-the-point?-ing pretty much anything anyone asked her to do. "What is the point," the long form of her argument went, "since all of civilization is

29

a waste, and everything is just random nothingness anyway?"

Usually Waylon argued with her. *The point is, right this minute scientists are figuring out hundreds of things that will make the world even more awesome than it already is. Telepathic communication! Human gills! Hover boards! Bionic body parts!* he might have said today. But he didn't.

"I need you," he repeated. "Come with me." He held his breath. Nobody ordered Neon around these days.

She dropped her head and exhaled, long and sizzly, like a volcano cooking lava. Waylon knew it wasn't lava she was cooking. But it was something just as hot: the Glare.

He braced himself. If Neon turned the Glare on in a grocery store, bacon would start to fry right in the package.

She lifted her head and aimed the Glare. Waylon felt his skin start to blister, but he took her hand and pulled her all the way down to the bottom of the stairwell.

"Is this about Arlo and the stupid teams?" she snarled when they got there. "I've told you: ganging up is stupid."

"No. It's about teleportation," he said. "I think I've achieved it."

Neon shot him a disbelieving eye roll and turned to leave.

"No, wait! Cells are made of atoms, and atoms rearrange themselves all the time!" Waylon told Neon about hearing the tiny buzzy sounds of himself living, and then . . . not. "I

31

think all my cells are de-materializing and then re-materializing somewhere else for split seconds. I need you to watch to see if I disappear. Don't blink."

Before she could argue, Waylon jumped under the stairs and clamped on the earmuffs.

Neon heaved a withering sigh, but then she squatted beside him and propped her eyes open with her fingers.

And it happened again. First, Waylon heard himself living, then every few seconds . . . he didn't. "So?" he asked.

"So nothing. You didn't go anywhere." Neon stood up.

Waylon scrambled out. "Maybe you missed it. You try, and I'll watch." He shoved the earmuffs at her. "Please?"

Neon gave Waylon another eye roll, but she clamped on the earmuffs.

Waylon watched hard. His sister didn't disappear.

But after a few minutes, the corners of her mouth twitched. One after the other, they lifted the slightest degree. Waylon realized her lips were trying to smile, something he thought they were no longer capable of.

"So?" he asked. "Did you hear your living-sounds? Did they disappear?"

Neon nodded. She looked dazed, but definitely happy.

Waylon, on the other hand, didn't know how he felt. He hadn't blinked once. He was positive Neon hadn't rearranged herself anywhere. No teleportation, which was a pretty big disappointment.

On the other hand, knowing that she'd had the same experience made him feel surprisingly great. These days, Neon seemed determined to live in a different world, locked in her room, typing away on a secret project nobody was even allowed to ask about.

Waylon missed his sister. A lot.

He sank down beside her. "What do you think it is?"

"You've discovered the negative void of doom," she told him in an impressed voice. "It's devouring us little by little from the inside. Nice work."

3

Wednesday morning, something happened that made everybody completely forget about teams for the day. Just as Mrs. Fernman was handing out the spelling lists, there was a knock on the door.

Waylon's third grade teacher, Mr. D'Matz, stood outside with Principal Rice. They looked grim as they beckoned Mrs. Fernman into the hall.

At first, even the kids who climbed onto their desks couldn't see anything except the three grown-ups' backs, huddled together. When the huddle broke, the kids in the front row passed the word that Mrs. Fernman's face was as white as the papers she still clutched, and her other hand was patting her chest, as though telling her heart to calm down.

Clementine went to the door and fake-sharpened her pencil. "'Disaster Boiling,'" she reported as she hurried back to her seat. "That's all I heard, but it was definitely a threat. Mrs. Fernman's in big trouble."

The door opened. Mrs. Fernman was pale and shaky, but she wore a smile. The smile looked painful, though, as if someone had nailed her lips open.

"Class," she said, "a new student will be joining us tomorrow."

Later, waiting for the buses, all anybody could talk about was the new kid. New kids were always popping in and out of classes, no big deal, but this one coming seemed different. Why did Mrs. Fernman have to warn them about it? What kind of a threat was Disaster Boiling? And why was Mr. D'Matz involved?

"Maybe it's his new baby," Rasheed said. "Yesterday he was bragging about how smart it is—maybe he's trying to get his new baby into fourth grade."

"I hope not," said Charlie. "Kid geniuses are one thing. Diapers are a whole 'nother story."

Everybody laughed at that, but it was kind

39

of a nervous laugh. More kids offered suggestions, but nothing seemed likely until . . .

"Maybe it's Baxter," Clementine said.

And the crowd of kids went silent.

"Maybe he's coming back," Clementine went

on, "and Mr. D'Matz was warning Mrs. Fernman about him."

Waylon's lunch lurched in his stomach.

Baxter had only been in third grade for a few days last September, but a couple of days were enough. When he'd left, the rumor was that he'd been sent away to prison. Everyone had agreed that it would be a good place for him.

"Well, you have to admit," Clementine said, "we were never bored those days he was in our class."

"He was a juvenile delinquent, Clementine!" Waylon cried. "We were never bored because we never knew what *crime* he was going to commit next."

Clementine's mouth dropped open. "Creamed corn in the soap dispenser? Clocks running backward? Those weren't crimes.

They were pranks—great ones. Baxter's really resourceful."

"Being resourceful isn't such a great recommendation," Waylon said. "Viruses are resourceful. There's one that wants to live inside a cat's brain, but it can't get inside a cat, so it's figured out a way to get inside a mouse's brain instead. It makes the mouse not afraid of cats. So the virus gets into the mouse, the mouse thinks, 'Oh, yawn, here comes a cat, whatever,' and the cat *eats* the mouse, and then—boom!—the virus is inside the cat. What if Baxter's resourceful like *that*?"

When Waylon stopped to catch his breath, he noticed that Arlo Brody had taken a step back and was eyeing him the way Waylon's father eyed a tomato in the market: as if he was worried about rotten spots. "Anyway," he tried, "what about that 'Disaster Boiling' threat you heard? Are you forgetting about that?"

Clementine scuffed the ground. "Well . . . Baxter's last name was Boylen. *Maybe* I didn't hear 'Disaster Boiling'—*maybe* what I heard was 'It's Baxter Boylen' instead."

Just then, Clementine's bus pulled in and she got on.

Waylon's bus was next in line, but for a long minute he stayed rooted to the school steps. If what Clementine really had heard was "Baxter Boylen," it would definitely be a threat.

4

It was Baxter, all right.

Principal Rice delivered him after the Pledge and then took off fast, as if she'd just remembered she'd left her office on fire.

"Is that a *beard*?" Charlie jumped up and demanded.

Waylon had been so transfixed by the jagged scar streaking across Baxter's face that he hadn't noticed the beard. *Knife fight*, that scar practically shouted. *Prison. You should see the other guy.* But Charlie was right—the lower half of Baxter's face was peppered with black speckles.

Mrs. Fernman shot Charlie a look, but you could tell she was biting her tongue against the beard question, too. "Class," she managed through clamped teeth, "please welcome our new student, Baxter Boylen. Some of you may remember him from Mr. D'Matz's class last year."

Some of the kids sure did remember him, and anyone passing by room 4B would've had no trouble picking out who they were. They were the ones flattened against the backs of their chairs like paint. Their eyes skidded all over the room as if they were searching for something desperately important—jewels, maybe, or one of their lungs. They looked everywhere except at the new kid sauntering to the empty desk in the back row.

The other half of the class dared to sneak peeks, but nothing too obvious. They'd heard the rumors.

Mrs. Fernman took advantage of the nervous silence to launch into a lesson on arctic tundras, and for the first time all year, nobody fell asleep behind a geography book. Half an hour later, when she turned her back to erase the board, Waylon risked a look.

Baxter slouched across his chair, eyes closed. The scar, bright pink and ropy, zigzagged up his cheek. As Waylon studied it, Baxter lifted his hand and slowly peeled it off his cheek. He rolled it into a ball and popped it into his mouth. Then he opened his eyes, stared directly at Waylon, and chewed.

Waylon suddenly knew how a cobra's prey felt, hypnotized by a cold, snaky gaze. Even when Baxter blew a big pink bubble, Waylon could not tear his eyes away.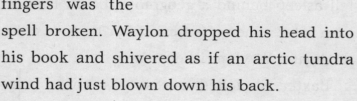

Only when Baxter popped the bubble with a flick of his fingers was the spell broken. Waylon dropped his head into his book and shivered as if an arctic tundra wind had just blown down his back.

Baxter didn't come outside for recess because, just before the bell, Principal Rice barged in and called him to follow her to her office for "a little welcoming chat." For the first time all week, the boys didn't separate into teams. In fact, nobody separated from anybody else, not even the boys from the girls. Everybody from 4B stood together whispering.

"He's twelve, at least. Maybe fifteen."

"I heard he rode a motorcycle to school. Which he stole."

"And that scar!"

"It was fake," Waylon explained. "I saw him roll it off his cheek and chew it."

"How do you know it was fake? How do you know he didn't pick off his scar and chew that?" Rasheed challenged.

"It was *gum*. He blew a *bubble* with it."

"Doesn't talk, been away for a year, eats flesh . . . he's a zombie," Charlie said. "He was away for zombie training." He raised his arms and lurched around in a circle, lunging at the other kids with his teeth bared. "Chomp, chomp, chomp."

"There's no such thing as zombies," Waylon said. Which he was almost sure was true.

"We'll tell that to your family when they

have to gather up your chewed-up zombie-spit-slimy body parts," Charlie said.

Waylon clutched his jacket tight in spite of himself.

Just before Waylon went to bed that night, Neon banged his door open.

"So?" She flopped down beside him on

the bed with a shrug that said *I don't see the point, but I'll ask anyway*. "Are you on a stupid team?"

Waylon nodded. "Arlo put me on the Shark-Punchers Tuesday."

"So now you're at war with the other team?"

"Not yet. This new kid came, and that's all anybody could talk about."

"Come on. Even Arlo the Great? Some new kid shows up, and he forgets he's plotting World War Three?"

"He did today, at least. Actually, Baxter's not really new. He was here for a few days last year, then he went to prison in Kansas."

Neon rolled her eyes and scoffed. "Kids don't go to prison. Is that what he says?"

"He doesn't *say* anything this year."

Neon dropped the bored act. "He doesn't talk?"

Waylon shook his head. "Not a word. He just came in all bad-acting with a beard, and he had a big scar, which I know was actually bubble gum, because I saw him peel it off."

"Huh," Neon said. Twice. She got up and tossed a pillow at Waylon. "Maybe you should leave him alone."

Waylon recalled Baxter's cold snaky gaze,

and how terrified it had made him feel. "Don't worry," he promised. "I will!"

"Maybe Arlo should, too."

"Fat chance. But Baxter's pretty scary, so I bet Arlo will put him on the Other team, away from me."

"Well, unless he decides he doesn't want such a scary guy on the opposite team," Neon said as she left.

Waylon pulled the pillow over his head. Fourth grade was shaping up to be a mess.

5

The scar and the beard were gone Friday, but everything about Baxter still said *Stay away!* He lounged in his seat with his eyelids lowered exactly halfway—open just enough that Mrs. Fernman couldn't accuse him of sleeping, and closed just enough that all the kids understood he wasn't paying the slightest bit of attention to her. His eyes flickered back and forth, as though he were watching a movie playing on the insides of those lowered lids.

Probably an R-rated movie, Waylon thought.

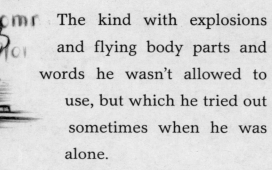

The kind with explosions and flying body parts and words he wasn't allowed to use, but which he tried out sometimes when he was alone.

That would be a brilliant idea, Waylon had to admit. *Invent internal movie projector, watch movies in secret whenever bored* would be a pretty great entry for his new life's work journal.

"Students," Mrs. Fernman called, pointing to the big blue words on the board: SAFE COMMUNITIES MONTH, "I expect by now you've each decided on your Community Safety Suggestion. Would anyone like to share it with the rest of the class?"

As Mrs. Fernman's gaze swept the room,

Waylon looked down and pretended to study his fingernails. He had lots of ideas for making things more awesome—his new journal was going to be full of them—but nothing yet for making things safer. *Safer* and *More Awesome* were pretty much opposites, he suddenly realized.

"I think we should give teachers 'Teacher on Board' signs for their cars. That would keep teachers safer, and teachers are the most valuable members of our community!" said Kayley-Anne. She beamed an angelic smile at Mrs. Fernman, fluffed her dress, and then sat down.

Fingernails, Waylon reminded himself as he stared harder at his, keep growing after a person dies. *The Science of Being Human*, Chapter Ten, "Corpse Curiosities." Which meant that if zombies were real, which they probably definitely weren't, they might have really long sharp claws. If zombies were real, getting rid of them would make the world both Safer *and* More Awesome.

Charlie raised his hand and said that the community would be safer if kids stayed home from school and watched television all day. That got a laugh, but Waylon thought it was actually a good suggestion—he sure would have felt safer at home this week.

Mrs. Fernman didn't see it that way. "That's enough sharing for today," she decided. "On Monday we'll write our reports. Tuesday, we'll make posters in Art. And on Wednesday we'll present our excellent suggestions at the police station."

At that, Baxter Boylen's head snapped up so sharply you could actually hear it. Everybody spun around to stare.

"Excuse me, Mrs. Fernman," he said, as if he were used to participating in class all the time, "we're going to the *police station*?"

All through recess, kids zipped back and forth across the playground sharing theories about why Baxter had suddenly come to life. Baxter himself slouched alone against the school wall, coolly eyeing all the zipping back and forth as if it were a Ping-Pong match.

Waylon eyed it too, sticking close to Arlo and listening carefully as the king learned pieces of gossip from his subjects.

"I bet he wants to steal a cruiser," Maria guessed. "Last year he told me he could hot-wire a car."

"We sure wouldn't want someone like that

59

on our team, would we?" Waylon asked after Maria zipped away.

Arlo surprised him. "Hmmm . . . You'd have to be pretty smart to hot-wire a car," he said as he squinted over at Baxter. "Maybe he could give my team some battle strategies. On the other hand, what if he steals my battle strategies?"

"Baxter drew a picture of a jail cell right after he learned about the police station," Rasheed said. "Maybe he's been in one before."

That didn't decide Arlo, either. "Was it any good?" Arlo asked. "Maybe my team could have a second logo, for when we do stuff. Like, 'Look out, we're putting the Others in jail.'"

Even when Charlie reminded everyone that last year Baxter had stolen his sandwich and hidden it so well no one found it until May, Arlo didn't make up his mind. "Well, maybe not everyone should be on a team" was all he said.

When the bell finally rang, Waylon still didn't know what Arlo was going to do. King Arlo was taking his time issuing his royal decree about Baxter. But that wasn't all.

Waylon had stood right beside Arlo all recess long. But not once did Arlo refer to the Shark-Punchers as "our team." Every time, it was "my team."

Was it his imagination, or was Arlo reconsidering *him*?

And was it his imagination, or did that make him feel really anxious?

That night, Waylon cleared his microscope, his biography of Madame Curie, and his pigeon skeleton from his bedside table. The light from his rocket-ship lamp now spilled a perfect buttery yellow circle on the empty space.

Which wouldn't be empty tomorrow. For

weeks he'd given up his Saturday cupcake from Rosie's—chocolate with marshmallow frosting, three dollars each—to save for his journal. Now he could imagine the lamplight flashing off the special gold ink he was going to label it with:

SCIENTIFIC LIFE'S WORK OF

WAYLON JENNINGS ZAKOWSKI.

He lay back and smiled. His whole life, he'd known he was destined to do something so great, he'd be famous. Except for his parents, all the grown-ups he'd ever told had misunderstood. "You're going to fly and time-travel and turn into other things?" they would ask. "You're meant to be superhero?"

"No, a *science* hero," he used to explain patiently. "I'm going to control gravity, ride the time-space continuum, and transmogrify. Things like that."

Lately, though, he didn't bother correcting

them. Because maybe they were right: maybe a science hero *was* a superhero.

Just as Waylon turned off his light, his father knocked on the door and stuck his head in. "You were pretty quiet this afternoon, buddy," he said. "All week, in fact. Anything wrong?"

Waylon sank back into his pillow and sighed. "When you were in school, did everybody start ganging up on each other?"

Waylon's dad came in and sat at the end of the bed. "They did. I'd forgotten that. All the boys in my school ganged up in packs. Well, all except me. Nobody wanted a film geek in their group. Nobody!"

Even in the dark, Waylon could see that his dad was smiling, as if the memory made him happy. "Didn't that make you feel terrible?"

"At first, sure."

"And then?"

"And then I happened to find a beat-up camcorder in a secondhand shop, and I got obsessed with making a movie. I joined the local community theater so I could learn things—set design, lighting, acting—and there I met kids from all over the city. So then I had a bunch of new friends."

"And after that, you didn't care about the kids at your school?"

Waylon's dad leaned forward. "Well, here's the crazy thing: once word got out that I was making a movie, every single kid who wouldn't let me on his team before suddenly wanted to be part of it." He patted Waylon's foot and then got up. "See, buddy, being passionate about something attracts people. Does that help?"

"Sure, Dad," Waylon lied. "'Night."

Mr. Zakowski left, and for a long while afterward, Waylon lay awake, staring into the darkness. In galactic time, his father wasn't that much older than he was—only about thirty years. But in terms of helping with fourth grade problems, he might as well be from the Jurassic Period.

6

On Saturday mornings, everyone was supposed to pitch in so that the Zakowski home wouldn't look, as Mr. Zakowski put it, like a poster for a cheesy disaster movie. Each week, he gave this imaginary disaster movie a new title: *Attack of the Towering Dishes*; *Avalanche of Litter*; *Laundrogeddon!*

Actually, all Waylon's father really wanted was a clean kitchen. His writing studio was a little room with a glass door off the kitchen. In it, he typed drafts of his screenplay. One day this screenplay would be made into a blockbuster movie: a thriller, a drama, and a comedy—a *thramedy*—all in one. It would be so powerful, audiences would leave theaters shaking their heads in awe and saying they would happily have paid twice the ticket price to see a film that terrific.

First, though, he had to finish his screenplay. To do that, Waylon's father needed a tidy kitchen. Because seeing a mess when he happened to turn his writer's chair, he said, made it impossible to create.

Waylon hurried out of his pajamas. While he dressed, he heard the sounds of his family already at breakfast. As he wandered into the kitchen, though, it went silent. Not the good kind of silent, the kind that meant everyone was happily tucking into their food. The bad kind, the kind that makes you think the air will

shatter like glass and shear your
ears off.

Waylon shook out some
cereal and ducked low over
the bowl. He peered
around warily.

His father was
at the sink, rinsing a
plate. His mother stood beside him, pointing to
the trash can. Neon was hurling the Glare at
them both, chipping black nail polish off her
thumbnail with her front teeth.

"The trash, Charlotte," Mrs. Zakowski tried
brightly, as though Neon were still a normal,
helpful kid who answered to her real name
these days. "It's your chore this week."

"What," Neon muttered after spitting some
nail polish specks onto the back of her wrist
and studying the effect, "is the point?"

"We don't want this place to look like a poster for *Revenge of the Rotting Rubbish*," Mr. Zakowski answered with a hopeful chuckle.

"But *what*," she asked with a long sigh, "is the *point*?"

"So we don't attract rats, is the point!"

Waylon looked up. Had his mother's voice just cracked?

"Right. So they don't overrun this place and gnaw off our feet while we're sleeping is the point," Mr. Zakowski tried, with a longing glance into his writing room.

Normally, Waylon loved imagining possibilities. But discovering that his feet had been gnawed off to bloody nubs while he was sleeping was an exception.

Still, he kept silent, munching his cereal and hoping that just this once, Newton's Third Law of Motion wouldn't kick in.

Newton's Third Law of Motion states that *Every force has an equal and opposite force in reaction.* Neon was a force, all right. When Mr. and Mrs. Zakowski pushed back against this force, the argument could go on for a while. But ultimately, both parents' equal and opposite reaction to Neon was to run.

Newton's Third Law held.

Mr. Zakowski crumbled first. "Hmmm . . . overrun by rats . . . middle of the night . . ." and he backed into his studio as if an idea this fresh had to be added immediately to his screenplay. Which now, Waylon figured, might actually *be* a cheesy disaster film.

Mrs. Zakowski was right behind him. Her eyes got the faraway glaze that meant she was dreaming about the nice, obedient medical robots in her lab. She turned to Waylon, silently begging him to take out the trash.

Waylon got up and tugged out the trash bag. Because sparring with their parents was only a warm-up for Neon, and as Newton had discovered centuries ago . . . what was the point?

After he'd taken out the trash, Waylon made his regular Saturday morning call to Joe. "What time should we take Buddy to the park today?" he asked.

There was a minute's silence at the other end of the phone. "Well . . . um . . . you know the rules."

"What rules?"

"Arlo's rules. If you're a Shark-Puncher, we can't hang out anymore."

"Oh," Waylon said. There was another long minute of silence before he spoke again. "Well, can I take Galaxy to the park by myself?"

"Sorry," Joe said. "Galaxy knows the rules, too. So, 'bye."

Waylon dialed Matt next. "Can we feed the penguins today?"

"I'm going to the aquarium later," Matt said. "But . . . um . . . you're not on the list."

"The list?" Waylon asked.

"Arlo's list. The Shark-Punchers."

"I'm not on it? That's just a mistake."

"Maybe," Matt said. When he hung up, the click hurt Waylon's ears.

7

On the way to the office supply store on Saturday afternoon, Mrs. Zakowski asked Waylon why he needed a journal. He told her.

Recording scientific accomplishments was something Mrs. Zakowski understood. She smiled. "Ah. Discoveries. Like Archimedes!"

Waylon skidded to a stop. "No, Mom! Definitely *not* like Archimedes!"

"Why not? He was one of the greatest scientists of all time. He was famous."

"He was famous all right—for being *naked*!

Don't you feel sorry for him? He figured out an important principle in a bathtub, and he's in all the history books running through the streets naked. I'm going to be famous too, but I am *not* going to discover anything in a bathtub."

"Well, technically, you take showers," his mother pointed out. "And you can never predict when a big idea is going to hit you. So, what kinds of discoveries will you be putting in this journal?"

"Everything. I've got lots of ideas. Lately, I've been concentrating on gravity."

"Gravity?" Mrs. Zakowski looked puzzled. "But Newton and Einstein have already covered that pretty thoroughly."

"Well sure, but don't you think gravity's got potential? What if you could counteract it, or turn it off and on, or tell it where to go?"

Waylon started imagining some of the things

he could do if only he could get gravity to loosen its grip. Like make the ball come to him in any sport. And couldn't he attract as many cupcakes—chocolate with marshmallow frosting, three dollars each—as he wanted? Best of all, Neil deGrasse Tyson, greatest living scientist—and probably greatest living human being—in the whole world, would probably want to meet him if he could control gravity. He was so excited about this last possibility that he almost missed what his mother said next. Almost.

He skidded to a stop again. "What do you mean, 'Gravity is *enough by itself*'???"

"I mean, gravity is. We factor it in to everything we do, every minute of every day. Look." She pointed to a roof overhang in front of them. "See those pigeons? We're going to walk *around* that ledge and not under it because we know that things *fall down*. What more do you want?"

Waylon started walking again. His mother studied how things *were*. He wanted to explore how things *could be*. They were worlds apart. But then it struck him: in that space between them was a perfect Community Safety Suggestion.

He looked back at the pigeons. Yes. A safety suggestion that would not only avert minor accidents, but also serious injuries. It could maybe even save lives. Actual lives. People received medals for doing that, and got television interviews.

Waylon didn't want a medal. But a television interview would go a long way toward making him famous. And not in a bathtub naked.

When they got to the store, Mrs. Zakowski

left Waylon alone, pretending she needed to pick up some stuff for her lab. Waylon knew she was pretending because he'd seen her lab. Everything in this store must look like an antique to her. But he appreciated the privacy.

One by one, he picked up every journal and studied it.

And finally he found it.

The journal was gray—a good, serious color.

It was just the right size— narrow enough to fit into his pocket, but thick enough to hold lots of ideas.

The cover was fake leather, which was good for two reasons: First, he didn't want to feel guilty about any cows dying. Second, fake leather was waterproof. If he had the bad luck of being in the shower when he had the good luck of discovering something great, at least he wouldn't have to worry about getting it wet.

But the best thing about this journal was the little brass lock on the cover. Waylon's ideas were extremely powerful, and who knew what could happen if they fell into the wrong hands.

He strode up the aisle and laid it on the counter along with two ten-dollar bills. "This is my journal," he told the clerk.

The clerk took Waylon's money and handed him back some change. "It is now," he agreed.

That night, Waylon went to his room as soon as *Miracles of the Natural World* ended. He opened his new journal and filled three pages with idea after brilliant idea.

Through the wall, he could hear Neon typing away, and that made him nearly as happy as writing in his journal did. Even if she didn't know it, they were still doing something together.

8

On weekends, Mr. and Mrs. Zakowski switched places. Waylon's father went out to work, while his mother stayed home.

Once Mr. Zakowski had made the big mistake of calling Saturday and Sunday his wife's days off. "Days off? Days *OFF*???" she had sputtered. That particular weekend had involved a bottle of scarlet nail polish spilled over a new white couch; tadpoles dumped into a toilet; a kid running away to the Boston Public Library; and, she claimed, close to a hundred diaper changes.

Waylon didn't like hearing about that time, since, as the younger kid, he had been responsible for only the diapers. But he did like switcheroo weekends. First of all, it was nice to have his mother home. Even better, his father usually invited Waylon to come along when he went to work, and Waylon always did. Mr. Zakowski's motto was *Monotony is the enemy of creativity,* so his jobs were always really interesting.

This weekend, Waylon hoped his dad was going to be a living statue in Boston Common. Of all his father's jobs, Waylon liked this one best, because the park was always full of dogs.

"Ben Franklin?" Waylon asked at breakfast Sunday morning.

"Yes, I'm feeling like Ben today. Two o'clock good, partner?"

"Two o'clock," Waylon agreed. He looked

84

over at his sister, hunkered over her toast. "Want to come with us?"

Neon didn't bother What's the point?-ing him. She only glowered and took her plate into her room. In a minute, Waylon heard the quiet but sharp clicks of her keyboard.

Waylon's father gazed at Neon's empty place at the table. From the look on his face, Waylon suspected that he missed Charlotte Brontë Zakowski just as much as he did. On the way to Boston Common, Waylon asked him about it.

Mr. Zakowski smiled, but he rubbed the little bald spot on the back of his head, which, Waylon knew, meant that he was sad. Waylon reached up and patted his arm.

"She doesn't play Lonelyville anymore. Remember how hard she used to laugh when she played Lonelyville?"

Years ago, Mr. Zakowski had written a script

for a TV movie called *Return to Lonelyville*. In it, a mean woman's doctor told her she was dying. Louise Pembleton decided to be nice so she could get some friends before she died. But it turned out the doctor was wrong; Louise *wasn't* going to die after all. She told all her new friends she wasn't going to die, thinking they'd be happy since now she could have a long life with them. But instead, they got mad because they thought she'd tricked them, so they left her alone again. Which made her mean again.

Lonelyville was a pretty terrible movie, and Mr. Zakowski said it had a lot of lines he'd just as soon forget he'd written, but the Heartstrings Channel showed it often because it was such a tearjerker. *So* often that Waylon and his sister could recite whole scenes of dialogue, which Mr. Zakowski did not find hilarious, but which Neon sure did.

"Really? Her playing Lonelyville? That's what you miss most?" Waylon asked.

"No, it's just what I happened to think of at this minute. I miss everything." He stopped, a serious look on his face. "Charlotte is going through a perfectly normal transition. It's like in a screenplay—by the end of Act One, the main character has to take on a new aspect of her persona in order to deal with the big challenges coming in Act Two. You understand?"

Waylon didn't—he almost never did when his dad got all writery—so he changed the subject. "What do you think about gravity?"

Mr. Zakowski gave Waylon the same puzzled look his mother had given him at the question. But after a minute, he said, "You know, it's a great metaphor. About the pull we can feel toward people. In fact, I think I'll put it in my screenplay. Dallas can tell her co-worker,

'You're affecting my gravity. I'm wobbling off course.' Or no, even better! In the love scene, Roberto will say, 'Your attraction is so strong, I'll orbit you forever!'"

Waylon knew his father was off, and there was no pulling him back—not without extra gravity, anyway. He picked up his dad's suit-case and headed into the park.

At a promising intersection of two busy paths, Waylon helped his dad get into his costume: tugging the skinny kneesocks up to the baggy britches, buckling the shoes, buttoning the hundreds of buttons on the vest and greatcoat. All the clothes had been spray-painted the same marble-gray color.

He carefully painted his dad's face and hands with marble-gray makeup, then watched while Mr. Zakowski put on a marble gray–painted wig and a marble gray–painted tricornered hat and marble gray–painted spectacles.

The effect amazed Waylon every time. "Dad?"

"Still in here."

Then Mr. Zakowski climbed onto a marble gray–painted box and struck a pose.

The trick to being a living statue isn't holding perfectly still. Anybody can do that with a

little practice. No, Waylon had noticed that the trick is knowing when to move for maximum effect. A well-timed wink could make people passing by jump and laugh. And then gather around and dig in their pockets for tips. You'd be amazed at how much money people will pay someone for standing around doing practically nothing.

His father bowed at a baby in a stroller, and the baby's parents jumped. Then they laughed and dropped a dollar into the hat beside the box. Before half an hour had gone by, the hat was brimming. Waylon emptied the money out, leaving a couple of singles and a five to give people the idea that this wasn't some nickel-and-dime show, and then took off to find a good place to play Want This Dog?

Waylon stretched out on an empty bench with a view of the park. He would never have

a dog—ever—because his mother was deathly allergic. But that didn't mean he couldn't pretend. Whenever a dog went by, he imagined that its owner was trying to give it away. *No thanks*, he imagined himself saying to a woman with a poodle. *Too fluffy*.

No, he thought when a teenager tugged a Saint Bernard past his bench. *Too slobbery*.

Playing Want This Dog? made him both sad

and happy at the same time. It hurt to see all those dogs he could never have. The truth was, he would have loved to take any of them. Still, it made him feel strangely happy that in all the times he'd played, he had never imagined himself answering *Yes*.

If he didn't know better, he could believe that the perfect dog—the one meant just for him—was waiting out there. But waiting for what, he couldn't imagine.

9

That night, Waylon had a hard time falling asleep. He'd ignored the whole team problem all weekend, but tomorrow it would be back. Arlo was either going to put him on the Shark-Punchers, which he would hate, or he wasn't, which somehow he would hate more. Even worse, what if Arlo put him on a team with Baxter? Worst of all, what if Arlo decided that both he and Disaster Boiling shouldn't be on a team at all?

He flipped on his lamp to study the History

of the Universe poster across the room. Usually, looking at it made him feel happy. On the left was the Inception—what most people called the Big Bang. All that energy bursting out at once must have been pretty thrilling, and Waylon was really glad it had happened.

Tonight, though, it struck him: he was living through his own personal Big Bang. Arlo had divided the fourth grade boys. Neon was shooting away from the family. When he could see himself from the outside, he even felt as if he might be separating from himself. Everything in his universe was exploding away in different directions.

He looked at the tiny image in the far left of the poster. He had never before wondered how the *singularity*—the compact ball of matter that was the universe before it expanded—had felt when the Big Bang happened.

Did the singularity feel lonely from all that whizzing away?

Because he sure did.

Did it wish everything would go back to the way it was before?

Because he sure did.

Just then, he heard a scratch at his door and a "Woof!"

Waylon smiled. Neon hadn't played Dog for a long time. Actually, Neon had never played it. Dog was strictly a Charlotte game.

When he was little he'd wanted a puppy so badly, his whole body had ached. Mrs. Zakowski had tried, but when they'd walked into the shelter, she'd had such a sneezing fit that she set all the animals to howling.

And that was when he'd really understood. No dog. Ever.

That night, Charlotte had scratched at

Waylon's door. She'd bounded into his room on all fours and barked and rolled over. Waylon had laughed so hard he'd finally stopped crying.

Now, Neon flopped onto the end of his bed. "Hey. Play OAT."

"No. I don't feel like it tonight."

Neon punched his foot. Fake hard. Not hard at all. "Play OAT."

"All right." He sighed. "One Awesome Thing: this afternoon, I saw three ants carrying a peanut. A whole peanut. I looked it up—if humans were that strong, three people could carry around the Statue of Liberty."

Neon rolled over. "That's better. And . . . ?"

Waylon knew what he was supposed to say now. He was the one who had invented OAT, and the one who insisted everyone say the same thing at the end, every time. He turned to the

wall. "I can't," he whispered. "I don't believe it anymore." He imagined hot desert winds blowing on his eyeballs. This worked to dry the tears that were threatening.

Neon punched him again. Still fake hard, but kind of hard for real, too. "Say it!" she growled, a pretend-furious dog now.

Waylon lifted his hand and traced over the symbols at the bottom of the periodic table hanging over his bed. Usually the heavier elements made him feel better. But tonight, not even Np, neptunium, or Pu, plutonium, gave him any strength. "I can't, Neon. Tomorrow's going to be really bad. The team thing." Saying it out loud made it worse. He pressed the heels of his palms into his eyes.

"It's stupid not to cry, you know. Everybody cries."

Waylon knew this, of course. *The Science of Being Human*, Chapter Seven, "People Plumbing." Still, he shook his head.

Neon gave him one more punch, this time so soft it felt like some kind of present. "All right," she said with a dramatic sigh. "Just this one time, I'll say it for you: *And* . . . tomorrow is going to be Even! More! Awesome!"

Waylon reached up and snapped off his lamp. "Sure. Even more awesome."

10

Monday morning, the Big-Bang, Everything-Is-Exploding-Away sensation was worse. Waylon's new journal, tucked deep in his jeans pocket, felt like the only thing holding him together.

The feeling didn't disappear when he got to school. "You may sit down, Waylon," Mrs. Fernman said at the end of the Pledge. "We're finished."

"I'm not," Waylon answered, his hand still over his heart, which felt like it could split apart if he didn't hold it together. "I'm still pledging." His words were as much a surprise to him as they seemed to be to Mrs. Fernman.

"Excuse me?" she stuttered.

"To the indivisible part. I think I need extra pledging about that. I'm feeling a little divisible today."

Mrs. Fernman tipped her head. She looked as if she were trying to translate what he had just said into a language she understood.

"Divisible—you know, like a cell in mitosis? Like an atom—nuclear fission?" he explained. "You can get started with whatever's next, and I'll catch up."

"I've been teaching fourth grade for thirty-nine years, and I've never had a student need more time with the Pledge!" Mrs. Fernman gave her head a little shake and then walked to her desk. "Class," she directed in a voice that still sounded a little confused, "please take out your geography books."

The feeling didn't disappear during Geography, either. Half the kids had dozed off behind their books by the time Mrs. Fernman got to "Isthmus: a narrow bridge of land that connects two larger land masses."

A couple more kids' heads hit their desks at that.

Not Waylon's. "That's *it*!" he wailed at the top of his lungs. "I'm an *isthmus*!"

That woke the sleeping kids, and they wanted to know what the still-awake kids were laughing about. Even Baxter Boylen had finally opened his eyes and was looking interested.

Waylon slumped onto his desk and covered his head. *Isthmus* was a hard word to say, and it was a dumb thing to blurt out in a classroom. He knew he should try to explain, or laugh at himself—anything for damage control.

But he couldn't. He was too busy trying to absorb what he had just figured out: his sister and his parents were like two large land masses drifting farther and farther apart. So were the Shark-Punchers and the Others. And he was the only bridge between them.

At recess, the Shark-Punchers and the Others retreated to opposite corners of the playground. While Waylon stood midway between, trying to decide what to do, Baxter came up to him.

"What's the deal with this Arlo guy?" he asked. "I heard about the team thing. How come he decides everything?"

Waylon took a step away, but he answered. "Are you kidding? Look at him." Waylon gazed

at Arlo along with Baxter, trying to see him through a stranger's eyes. It was pretty obvious: Arlo was big and strong and handsome, and he had that crown-hair thing going for him. "He's great at everything. Plus, he's nice. Even the girls like him."

"So how come you're not on a team?"

Waylon took another step away. "I will be soon. Arlo's desperate for me to join."

"He is? So which are you, a jock or a brain?"

Suddenly Waylon realized it wasn't the jock or the brain that bothered him. It was the "or." Why not an "and"? Why not a "but also"?

"Neither," he said. "I'm an isthmus, remember?"

He turned his back and headed over to the Shark-Punchers' corner. When he got near, he raised his hand to wave at Arlo.

And Arlo turned away.

Arlo, the king of the whole school, turned away.

And at that instant, Waylon saw himself from the outside. What he'd done with his hand hadn't looked like a wave at all—it had looked like the pathetic last reach of an isthmus, right before it's swallowed up by the cold, dark sea.

Baxter stood against the wall, watching him. And suddenly Waylon knew—whatever it took, he had to get back on Arlo's team again.

He started a line to go back to class, even though the bell wouldn't ring for ten minutes. When the doors opened, he went straight to his desk and got to work on his Community Safety paper. His presentation was going to be great. So great that Arlo was going to say, *I want another brain on my team!* again. It had better be.

When Waylon got home, his father handed him the phone. "It's Mitchell," he said. "He's called three times already."

Waylon dropped his backpack, surprised. All year, he and Mitchell had had a deal. He had taught Mitchell the science behind baseball, and Mitchell had coached him through Little League. Waylon hadn't seen him since August, though.

"Hey, Science Dude," Mitchell said. "We're

studying atomic structure this week, and I really, really, really need your help."

Waylon felt himself glow brighter with importance with each "really"—Mitchell was fourteen and a star athlete. "Sure," he said, trying out a slightly deeper voice than normal. "Want to come over here?"

For a minute, there was a silence at the other end of the phone. "Well . . . I would, but . . . Okay, the thing is: is your sister there? Because, Science Dude, I gotta say, this year she's turned *scary*."

Waylon wasn't surprised to learn that Neon was scaring people at school, too. But it made him feel sad.

"She's not scary," he said. "She's really nice."

"Sure. And a rattlesnake makes an awesome pet. Is she there, or not?"

"She'll be home soon," Waylon admitted.

"Okay, then can you just help me over the phone?"

He could and he did. He explained protons, neutrons, and electrons and their orbits. All the time, though, he was thinking about his sister, orbiting away from everything she used to love.

After dinner, the Zakowski family sat down to watch a movie. Neon's spot on the couch seemed emptier than usual. When the show ended, Mr. Zakowski went in to say good night to her.

"Mom," Waylon asked, "do you miss the old Charlotte?"

Mrs. Zakowski sighed. "She used to let me braid her hair for hours. All these crazy patterns."

"That's what you miss most?"

She sighed again. "I miss how happy she used to be just hanging out with us. But she's a teenager now, Waylon. She's supposed to rebel—it's in her contract. Listen, it's a hard stage, but it's just a stage. She'll come through it."

"I keep thinking I should do something."

"Oh, no. Your only job is to be a good brother." She reached out and scrambled his hair. "Which you already are."

Waylon went to his room and lay down on his bed. He hoped his mother was right, that it was just a stage. But she was wrong that there was nothing he should do.

He was an isthmus. That was his job.

A lot was riding on him. No matter how stretched out it made him feel, he was going to have to keep spanning the gulf between Neon and his parents. Because if he didn't, his sister was going to end up an island.

11

Tuesday morning, it was right to Art after the Pledge.

Waylon liked Art all right, except for the dusty chalk. And the clay that wedged under his nails. And the paint that dried to an itchy crust over his fingers. Waylon didn't like touching things that weren't cool and dry, and there were lots of those things in the Art Room.

Actually, there were lots of them in the world, too. Waylon pulled out his journal. *Invent Teflon fingerskins,* he wrote with a nod.

115

"What did you just write in there?"

Waylon hadn't heard Baxter sneak up on him. "Nothing. There's nothing in there at all." He jammed the journal back into his pocket and scanned the room. If Arlo saw him talking to Baxter, it would ruin his chances.

Arlo was staring right at him.

Waylon grabbed a pack of cool, dry markers and hurried away from Baxter to a seat at the farthest table. He bit his lip and set to work drawing a poster that would show everybody, especially Arlo Brody, just how genius his Safety Suggestion was.

At recess, Waylon headed straight over to where the Shark-Punchers were kneeling in a circle, rolling pinecones through a mud puddle.

"Hey, Arlo, I was just wondering if you noticed I didn't blurt anything out today,"

Waylon said. "Also, I sure didn't stick around when that Baxter started bothering me in Art."

"Uh-huh." Arlo rolled another pinecone and added it to the stack.

"What are they for?" Waylon asked, although he could guess.

"Arsenal," Arlo answered. "I told the Others to stock up too. It's going to be cool."

Waylon said, "Wow, that sure sounds cool,"

even though it didn't. He wouldn't want to throw sticky, muddy pinecones at any of his friends, and he sure didn't want to be hit by any. "I can't wait."

But Arlo never even looked up.

When Waylon got home, he gathered his courage and knocked on Neon's door. "Arlo Brody has ruined fourth grade!" he yelled as soon as she opened it. "The only thing worse than having to be on a team is not having a team to be on! It's so stupid!"

He steeled himself for Neon's wrath, but instead, she slumped to the floor and patted her rug. Waylon sat beside her warily. He was stunned when she leaned her head on his shoulder.

"I know." She sighed. "And if you think fourth grade boys are bad, you should try eighth

grade girls. What kind of jeans are cool, which
boy is cute. Who sits with whom. Hairstyles
and celebrities. I can't stand that cabbage-head
stuff!"

"So what do you do?"

"This." She jumped up, turned on the Glare,
and flicked her black hair spikes. "Oh, yeah,
the cabbage-heads leave Neon alone. And then
I can concentrate on my project." Neon pulled
some papers from her printer and clasped them

to her chest. "Which is absolutely amazing. It's about life, how everything is connected and—"

"You've been writing a book?"

"No, it's more! It's got visual art, too, and film."

"Like a screenplay?"

"No, more. It's also got music, and dancing. And vibrations, so people feel it, too. It's about the Everythingness, so it has to take lots of forms."

Waylon tugged his hair at the temples, making room for what he was learning. "So . . . when you say everything is nothing, what you really think is that everything is *everything*?"

"Uh . . . yeah."

"And you're pretending to be someone you're *not*—someone scary—so people will leave you alone so you can be who you *are*?"

"Uh-huh. Exactly."

"Oh, wow! Batesian mimicry!"

"What?"

"Batesian mimicry—it's really cool. It's where a harmless species mimics a dangerous species to be left alone by predators. Like some species of moths that look like bees—nobody messes with them!" Waylon explained. "What about friends, though? Aren't you lonely?"

"Oh, I have friends. There's a group of us. We sit together at lunch and we work on the project after school. I'm meeting them in a few minutes. Having a great project is wonderful, but if you had to do it alone, well . . . what's the point?"

Hearing this, Waylon felt a little better. But only a little. "You should tell Mom and Dad that this is an act."

"They're our parents. They know. I mean, didn't you?"

Waylon stopped to consider it. "No. I wished it, but I didn't know it. Mom and Dad don't either. They know you're okay, but they really miss you." Waylon told her what each of them had said.

Neon stretched out her arms and wiggled her black fingernails. "I put a lot of effort into all this, and it's working."

"But Mom and Dad and me—we're not cabbage-heads."

Neon shrugged on her tattered black jacket. "I'll think about it."

An hour later, Mitchell called for another lesson on atoms. When Waylon told him Neon was gone until dinnertime, he heaved a huge sigh. "Okay, then, I'll come over. As long as the coast is clear."

For a minute, Waylon was tempted to tell

him the truth—that his sister was just pretending. Wouldn't it be great if Charlotte could have a friend like Mitchell? All three of them could do stuff together. . . .

Then his mother's words came to him: *Your only job is to be a good brother.*

And right now, that meant telling a lie.

"You're right about Neon, Mitchell," he said. "You should warn everyone to leave her alone."

"Wow, thanks, Science Dude. I will. See you in a few."

Mitchell only lived a few blocks away, so he really was there in a few minutes. Waylon started with the difference between electromagnetic force and nuclear force, and that went pretty well. But he had barely introduced quarks when Mitchell clapped his hands over his ears. "Stop! My brain's exploding!"

"Wait . . . seriously?" Waylon asked, trying

not to sound too eager. He pulled *The Science of Being Human* from his shelf and thumbed it open to Chapter Six: "Beyond Bizarre." "Maybe you have this: *Exploding Head Syndrome.* Are you hearing a really loud noise that isn't real?"

Mitchell laughed. "No, I just meant that's a lot of hard stuff. Isn't there anything fun about atoms?"

Waylon thought that everything about atoms was fun, but he knew what Mitchell meant.

"Actually . . ." he dropped his voice to imitate the *Miracles of the Natural World* host. It was the voice he always used whenever he told someone about this particular miracle of the natural world. "All the atoms that are here now have always been here. Since Earth was formed, four and a half billion years ago."

"There's no new stuff?" Mitchell asked.

"Well, once in a while, a meteor hits us or we pick up some space dust. But that hardly counts."

"And nothing leaves?"

"We shoot a little bit of stuff into space, but otherwise, no. And that means"—Waylon paused dramatically to pull out a piece of lint from his pocket—"an atom in this lint might once have been in a dinosaur's tooth. Or King Tut's fingernail."

Mitchell's eyes widened as it hit him.

"Science Dude, do you seriously mean my bat might contain an atom from Babe Ruth's bat?"

"Sure."

"Or, even *me*? Like, my hair might have once been Joe DiMaggio's hair?"

"Why not?"

Mitchell whooped and grabbed his hair. "I can never cut it! But wait . . . how can you tell if it is?"

"Well, you can't," Waylon said. "It's just a possibility."

At this, Mitchell's face collapsed. Waylon felt that somehow he was personally responsible. After Mitchell left, he drew out his journal. *Invent atom-history tracking,* he wrote. *Learn where all your atoms have been.*

Waylon held up his hand, trying to calculate how many atoms there might be in his body. There were ten million alone in a single fingernail. Ten million, each with its own secret history.

No wonder he blurted things out. This world was so amazing, how could anyone hold it all in?

12

The Shark-Punchers and the Others spent the entire ride to the police station shoving pinecones down each other's shirts and silent-shrieking in outrage. Baxter, clamped beside Mrs. Fernman in the front seat, and Waylon, sitting alone at the back of the bus, were the only boys who weren't a part of it.

Waylon watched, suffering from another divisibility problem. There was nothing half of him would enjoy less than having a muddy, sticky pinecone stuffed down his shirt. And there was nothing half of him wanted more.

When the bus pulled in to the police station, Mrs. Fernman stood up. "No horsing around inside," she reminded everybody. "In thirty-nine years of teaching I've never canceled a field trip, but I will if I have to." The class climbed off the bus quietly and lined up at the desk labeled DISPATCHER to be signed in.

"Waylon Jennings Zakowski," Waylon told the bored-looking officer when it was his turn. "Want me to spell it? For the medal?"

The bored-looking officer looked up. "Medal?" she asked.

"For my Community Safety idea," Waylon prompted, loud enough to be sure that Arlo, at the end of the line, heard. "Z-A-K—"

"Zakowski. I think I can figure it out."

"Well, my suggestion is really going to improve safety," Waylon went on. "You should probably call the TV station now so they can send someone over."

The dispatcher looked bored again. "Next," she said.

Next was Baxter. He held out his hand. "Want to fingerprint me?"

"That won't be necessary, Mr. Boylen," the dispatcher told him. "We already have yours on file, now, don't we?"

All the 4B kids gasped at that, and when Mrs. Fernman herded them into a meeting room for the presentations, their jaws were still hanging open.

The chief made a speech about Community This and Safety That—Waylon was too excited to catch the details. His moment was almost here. Arlo would see how smart he was and invite him back to his team.

Then everyone lined up at the podium. Most of the suggestions were pretty disappointing. Kids mumbled promises to follow bike rules, holding up posters of accidents. A *lot* of red paint had been used. After each, a bald-headed officer ushered them off the podium with a fake cheerful comment about how much safer Boston's streets were going to be.

Even the suggestions that weren't about bike safety were pretty lame. Marco's was about doubling up on potholders when taking really hot things out of the oven, and Willy's was about staying close to your sister on outings. Kayley-Anne stuck to her idea about TEACHER ON BOARD signs, and nobody, not even Mrs. Fernman, could muster more than a single clap. As she left the podium she added, "And I meant to say also, Police Officer On Board signs, too. Because police officers are the second-most important people in our community!" But even that didn't get a hand.

At each dull suggestion, Waylon got more and more excited—his contribution was going to blow everyone else's away. At last it was his turn.

He held his poster high, turning it so everyone could see: a smiling woman rolling a baby carriage. A piano hovered above her. The rays shooting out of the woman's hat left no doubt about how powerful they were.

"Things above us are especially dangerous," Waylon began. "My suggestion is a gravity-counteracting hat that—"

"Heh-heh, thanks for that, young man," the fake-cheerful officer interrupted. "Science fiction certainly is fun."

"It's *not* science fiction," Waylon said. "It could be done with magnets if the falling objects were magnetically charged. Or with jet propulsion, if you factored recoil into the hat. Or—"

"Young man, do you have a real suggestion?"

Waylon felt his cheeks burning. It was only the veins in his face dilating, he knew from *The Science of Being Human*, Chapter Four, "It Happens to Everyone." Blushing was one of the few design flaws in the human body—when you were embarrassed, wouldn't it be better for your cells to become transparent, so you could disappear?

Waylon pulled out his journal. But before he could jot down this excellent idea, the bald officer called, "Next, please!" not even bothering to act cheerful.

Waylon's cheeks flared hotter. As he stepped away, he suddenly saw himself from the outside again. *Is that a boy,* the mean kids in his imagination asked with nasty smirks, *or a roasted tomato?*

At least the real kids, the ones from his class, didn't smirk. But some looked as if they might have if they weren't in a police station.

Not Baxter. Baxter shot him a thumbs-up as he stepped up.

"There's a stop sign near my house," he began. "I tracked which cars came to a full stop and which didn't. I thought maybe sports cars would ignore the sign more often than minivans. But it didn't matter. All kinds were the same. Except for one."

"Yes, young fella?" the bald officer asked with a fake chuckle. "There's a certain kind of vehicle we should keep an eye on?"

Baxter nodded. "Police cruisers. Not a single one of them came to a full stop. In three hours

I saw nine cruisers only slow down and roll through. Our community would be a lot safer if our cops obeyed the stop signs. And so would our cops!"

"Thanks so much," the officer said, his head shining with sweat. "We'll have to wrap up now."

But Baxter wasn't through. "That's a zero percent cooperation rate," he said, and anyone who didn't know him would have sworn he was trying to be helpful. "Or you could call it a one hundred percent failure-to-stop rate. Either one."

As Baxter was dragged away from the podium, Waylon returned his thumbs-up. When the new kid talked, Waylon realized, he didn't seem that scary. In fact, he seemed kind of normal. And he had to admit, Baxter's suggestion would actually improve community safety.

Apparently, the police didn't see it that way. They gave Arlo Brody the prize, which was only a certificate. Probably his hair looked like a peaked police hat to the judges, Waylon thought.

As the class filed out, a tall policeman crooked his finger and called Baxter aside. The whispering started immediately.

"I bet he stole something while nobody was watching."

"They have his fingerprints on file!"

"He's probably been in jail there already."

"I heard one of them ask about his father. Maybe his father's in jail!"

That would explain a lot, everyone agreed.

Waylon drifted away and took the same seat at the back of the bus.

In physics, an "isolated system" was one so far removed from others that it wasn't affected by any external forces. That was him, Waylon realized—an isolated system. Destined to be alone. Doomed unfairly, like Louise Pembleton from Lonelyville, to a friendless life. Just as he was almost starting to enjoy the dramatic misery of this thought, an external force affected him.

"Waylon *Jennings*?" Baxter asked as he dropped to the seat. "Like the outlaw?"

For a minute, Waylon thought about changing

his seat. Then he realized that it didn't matter. His situation was hopeless now—the episode in the police station had doomed his chances to be a Shark-Puncher for sure.

"Waylon Jennings wasn't an outlaw," he said. "He was a country music star. See, my father named my sister after a hero of his. When I was born, it was my mother's turn," he recited. "Copernicus was her first choice, but my father said no to torturing any kid of his with a name like Copernicus Zakowski. He said the same thing about Galileo and Eratosthenes. Finally my mother threw up her hands and said, 'Fine, how about Waylon Jennings?' She listens to his music when she's working."

"So your mother is an outlaw?" Baxter asked.

"No! She's a medical robotics scientist!"

"Then it's your father who's the outlaw?" Baxter asked hopefully.

"No. Nobody in my family is an outlaw."

"Too bad," Baxter said, shaking his head. "It sure sounds like an outlaw's name."

In front of them, the pinecone-stuffing started up again. If he *were* an outlaw, Waylon thought, the very first thing he'd steal would be those stupid muddy pinecones.

13

The instant his eyes opened Thursday morning, Waylon sensed something was wrong.

His journal!

It wasn't on the bedside table.

Panic seized him. Panic, according to *The Science of Being Human,* Chapter Four, "It Happens to Everyone," was only a chemical reaction. The neurotransmitter adrenaline was preparing his body for Fight or Flight. Waylon understood the Flight response—he'd fly across the world if it would recover his journal. But Fighting always seemed dumb.

He pulled on yesterday's jeans and searched the pockets. It wasn't there.

He raced into the kitchen and checked his jacket and backpack. No journal.

He grabbed a muffin and ran out the door. It wasn't in the lobby and it wasn't on the bus and it wasn't in his locker and it wasn't in his desk.

All the way through Geography, Waylon kept patting his pocket. Its emptiness was a fresh loss every time. He gave Willy a silent nod of brotherhood. Phantom Anything Syndrome was no fun.

When recess came, Waylon tore around the playground, asking everybody if they'd seen it.

"No," everybody said. "Sorry."

At lunch, everything the cafeteria ladies slapped on his plate made him feel worse. The chicken patty had the same fake-leather look as his journal. The potato puffs were the same gray color. The string beans were grayish, too, and they all seemed to be pointing at him like fingers, blaming him for being careless.

He felt a tray poke his ribs from behind. "What's the big deal with this journal, anyway?" Clementine asked.

Waylon set his tray on a table and slumped

onto the bench. "It was for recording my scientific life's work in. I was going to send it to Neil deGrasse Tyson when it was full. But now it's gone."

Clementine straddled the bench across from him. "You should write your important stuff on your arm, like I do. I never lose my arm." She rolled up her sleeve.

Get fake intestines for Halloween costume. Or real.

"I'm going to have too many discoveries for that," Waylon said. "I wouldn't have enough skin. Besides, they need to be more private."

"A journal's not private."

"Mine is." From under his shirt, he pulled out the key on its string.

Clementine looked impressed. "You have discoveries that need to be locked up? Like what?"

"Well, like controlling gravity, for one thing."

"You got something?" a new voice broke in. "On gravity?"

Waylon spun around. Baxter set his tray down beside him.

"Well, um . . . no. Not yet."

"He's going to," Clementine said.

Waylon kicked her under the table, but she didn't take the hint. "Waylon's the scienciest kid in the whole school," she went on. "Let me tell you, if anyone is going to be able to control gravity, it's him."

Baxter popped open his milk. "Would you be able to, say, jump over prison walls?"

Waylon exchanged a nervous look with Clementine at that. "Well . . . sure. You could jump over all kinds of high things."

Baxter nodded. "Think you're going to be able to do it soon? Like by Saturday?"

"Probably not," Waylon admitted. And then, although he had no intention of prolonging any discussion with Disaster Boiling, his mouth opened and said, "But if it's high jumping you need, controlling gravity's not the only way."

Baxter cocked his head, a carrot stick in midair. "You got something else?"

148

"*I* don't. Fleas do."

"Fleas?"

Waylon nodded. "A flea can jump one hundred and thirty times its own height. It's so amazing. If you were five feet tall, that would mean you could jump six hundred and fifty feet straight up and barely notice it. So the trick is to figure out flea mechanics and apply them to human legs."

"Huh. Science," Baxter mused. "Go figure."

"He's got lots of stuff like that," Clementine said. "His journal's full of it. But he lost it."

"That gray one? The one with nothing in it?" Baxter asked. "It's not lost." He picked up his grilled cheese and took a bite.

Waylon gaped at him. "You know where my journal is?"

Baxter took another bite. "Yep. You left it on the podium at the police station."

"How come you didn't tell me?"

Baxter shrugged. "You didn't ask."

Waylon looked down at his tray. And then away, because the string beans were pointing at him again, accusing him of something else. He'd asked every single boy on Arlo's team, every single boy on the Other team, and all the girls. The only person he hadn't asked was Baxter Boylen. He hoped Baxter didn't know this.

"You asked everyone else," Baxter said. "How come you didn't ask me?"

Waylon didn't answer. His silence sounded guilty.

Baxter got up and stuffed his chicken patty into his pocket. "I'll get it for you. I'm going there after school anyway, to visit my dad," he called over his shoulder as he left.

"Wow," Clementine said. "That was lucky."

Waylon's head sank to his hands. "It *would*

be lucky if it weren't Baxter," he groaned. He flashed his journal key again. "Remember his Teach-a-Skill presentation last year? Picking locks!"

"So go with him if you're worried."

"Are you kidding? You heard him. He's going there to visit his father. Sounds like he's trying to bust him out of jail."

Clementine shrugged as if busting a criminal out of jail was no big deal. For Waylon, though, it was. He tugged on his hair, but no solution came. He scraped his tray and then went to the office to call home for permission to walk.

"See you this afternoon," Mr. Zakowski said.

I sure hope so, thought Waylon as he hung up.

14

If Baxter was surprised to find Waylon following him after school, he didn't show it. After a few blocks, though, Baxter suddenly jumped up and slapped the sign by the Lucky Horseshoe Tavern. "Dutch Henry Borne was the biggest horse thief in the West," he said over his shoulder. "He once sold a sheriff his own horse."

Waylon jumped to slap the sign too. "Horses can't burp. A horse's digestive system is one-way only."

On the next block was a wall covered in

graffiti. Baxter went over and traced one of the words. "Jesse James never swore," he said. "When he was mad, he made up his own words. *Dingus* was his favorite."

Waylon pulled up beside Baxter, and without really meaning to, traced over one of the swears also. "People with Tourette's syndrome can't help swearing," he offered.

Rosie's Bakery was on the next block.

Waylon's mouth watered as they passed it. Seven weeks, no cupcake. Maybe this weekend.

Next to Rosie's was a bank. Baxter pressed his face to a window. "Pretty Boy Floyd once robbed the same bank twice."

Waylon looked in the window too. He tried, but he couldn't come up with a scientific fact about banks. "I give up," he said. "How come you know so much criminal stuff? Is it because your dad's in jail?"

Baxter's eyebrows nearly shot out of his forehead. "My dad's not in jail! He's a cop! And I know all that stuff because I helped him study criminal behavior."

"Oh." Waylon was quiet for a whole block as he sorted out this new information. "Everyone thinks *you're* a criminal. The way you act. Not talking. The scar, the beard."

"I know. I want them to."

"How come?"

Baxter shrugged. "It keeps people away. I have something really important to do. I can't be bothered with all that stupid team stuff right now."

"Huh." Waylon thought about his sister and smiled. "Batesian mimicry."

"What?"

"Nothing. But wait—why did you ask about jumping over prison walls if you don't know anyone in jail?"

"Oh, I do. Dumpster Eddy. I'm going to visit him today too. Here we are."

Baxter was right. The police station loomed up beside them, looking ominous now, like something from a horror film. "Dumpster Eddy?" Waylon gulped. "You're visiting a guy in jail named Dumpster Eddy?"

"Well, that's what I call him. He was nabbed in a Dumpster." Baxter smiled as if he admired the guy. "Bones all around."

Waylon shuddered. "What if your father finds out?"

"Oh, he knows. He's the one who put him behind bars."

"Wait. Your father is a policeman, and he lets you visit a criminal he arrested?"

"Dumpster Eddy's not a criminal. He didn't do anything wrong."

"Well, then, what's he in jail for?"

Baxter threw his hands up and shook his head sadly. "He was in the wrong place at the wrong time. And it gets worse. He's on Death Row."

"You're visiting a guy who's going to be executed?" Waylon gasped.

Baxter nodded. "His time's up on Saturday. Except"—Baxter ducked his head and lowered his voice—"this part my father doesn't know. I'm going to bust him out. You can help me."

"Oh, no. Nope. Nope." Waylon waved his hands and backed away. "I can't help bust a criminal out of jail!"

"I told you, he's not a criminal. He's a runner, is what he is. Long-distance, sprints—you name it, he was born to do it. It's his destiny. It just kills me to see him locked in a cell where he can't run."

For an instant, Waylon felt a flash of sympathy—sometimes at the end of a long day stuck behind his desk at school, his legs wanted to jump right off his body—but it was just a flash.

"Please," Baxter asked. "Just come scope out

the place, then tell me some science to get him out. That's all, I swear."

Waylon looked up at the station's big front doors. He felt too divisible again, right down the middle. On the one hand, he really didn't want to meet anyone called Dumpster Eddy. On the other hand, he really wanted his journal back.

He patted his empty pocket. And then followed Baxter up the steps.

Inside the lobby, Baxter asked for Officer Boylen. Right away, a tall man with Baxter's same curly hair came out from the back, grinning. His uniform was new and his badge was gleaming. "Hey, Bax!" the tall policeman said. "Who have you got with you?"

"Waylon. Jennings, like the outlaw. He left a notebook in the meeting room yesterday."

Officer Boylen left and was back in a minute with the journal. When Waylon curled his fingers around it, the lock still securely intact, his whole body relaxed. He tucked it deep into his pocket.

"Can we visit Dumpster Eddy?" Baxter asked.

Officer Boylen walked over to a steel door with a big padlock. He took a key from his chain and clicked the lock open. Waylon froze, but Baxter sauntered right in.

And the inmates went berserk, leaping into the air, pressing their faces through the bars . . . and *barking*.

"These are *dogs* in here!" Waylon cried, running down the row after Baxter. "Dumpster Eddy is a *dog*!"

Baxter was crouched at the last cage, hugging a scruffy brown dog through the bars. Dumpster Eddy wasn't just any dog, Waylon could see. He was a great dog. He had one black eye patch and his lips curled up in a lopsided dog-grin. He was not too small, not too big, not too fluffy, not too slobbery. He was a perfect

dog. *YES!* Waylon would say if he were playing
Want This Dog? for real, *YES! I DO!*

When Dumpster Eddy saw Waylon, he
started jumping straight up and down on his
stick-skinny legs and yipping his head off, as if
he were playing Want This Boy? and answering
YES! I DO!

Baxter pulled the chicken patty out of his pocket and fed it to Eddy bite by bite. Then he stood up. "Nobody claimed him. The police only keep them here for ten days—he's going to the shelter Saturday. He's not exactly the kind of dog people want. Kind of patchy. Plus, anyone could see he's a runner. No one's going to adopt him, so . . ." Baxter made a slicing motion at his neck, and Waylon shuddered.

Eddy watched as if he knew exactly what Baxter meant.

"I'd take him, but our apartment is No Pets." Baxter looked hopefully at Waylon.

Waylon felt a lump of longing grow in his throat as he shook his head. "My mom's allergic."

He knelt and stroked Eddy's ears. Eddy locked his gaze on Waylon's. And suddenly there were no bars between them. There was no boy skin; there was no dog fur. Waylon and

Dumpster Eddy grokked each other's souls in that steady look of Eddy's.

Get me out of here, that look said. *Set me free.*

That look stabbed Waylon right through the heart. He hadn't read about anything like this sensation in *The Science of Being Human.* But Baxter was apparently feeling it too. Tears bulged in his eyes.

Waylon stood up. "Everybody cries," he said. "I know."

"Well, did you know that if we were in space, at zero gravity, our tears would just pop out and go floating around?"

Baxter laughed and wiped his face. "No. That would be crazy," he said. "Thanks."

"You're welcome." And then Waylon simply stood beside Baxter, grokking the freedom-hungering dog-ness of Eddy.

"I could pick the lock to get in here, no problem," Baxter said at last, his voice low. "Then I could set him free through the back door. But there's always somebody at the dispatcher's desk." Baxter and Waylon looked back down the hall, and sure enough, the dispatcher waved.

"I need something else. Something science-y. Like gravity . . . you got any gravity stuff that would help?"

Waylon thought hard. "No. No gravity stuff. Teleportation would be ideal, but . . . I haven't quite perfected it yet."

"So that's it? The scienciest guy in school, and you don't have anything?"

Waylon tugged up tufts of his hair, over and over, until he figured he probably looked like he had spines.

Spines. And then he knew.

"The three-spined stickleback will pretend to be eating something delicious on the ocean floor to keep predators away from its nest. Shore birds fake a hurt wing." Waylon's voice rose with excitement. "A squid will drop one of its own arms and leave it glowing."

"So . . . ?" Baxter asked.

"So, distraction displays. They work. You need one."

"You think I should cause a distraction at the

same time I'm picking a lock and letting Eddy out? That's your brilliant idea?"

Waylon gave Dumpster Eddy a final head scratch. Then he turned to Baxter. "No. My brilliant idea is: You'll pick the lock and let Eddy out. Your *accomplice* will cause the distraction." He stuck out his hand to shake.

And Baxter took it.

15

The instant the bell rang for Friday recess, Waylon and Baxter shot out of their seats and grabbed up markers and paper. The Shark-Punchers and the Others were still trudging out to their corners of the playground when Waylon and Baxter burst past them to the play structure in the middle. They flopped down with their heads together. Waylon began a diagram of the police lobby, and Baxter started sketching the cages.

A few minutes later, a shadow fell over

Waylon's paper. He looked up. He hadn't heard them gathering, but bunches of kids now ringed the play structure. More boys from both teams were heading over, along with some girls, too.

Charlie bellied down the slide. "What are you guys doing?"

"Yeah," a chorus of other curious voices repeated. "What are you guys doing?"

Waylon and Baxter ignored them and got back to work. Recess was short, and Dumpster Eddy had only hours left to live. "Behind the cells there's a door to an alley," Baxter said. "That's where I'll take him."

Rasheed and Joe climbed the monkey bars and dangled down. "Are those *jail* cells?" Rasheed asked.

"With *dogs* in them?" Joe demanded.

Baxter and Waylon ignored them, too. Dumpster Eddy needed their whole attention.

170

Baxter pulled an old padlock and a bobby pin from his pocket and began practicing. Waylon wrote POSSIBLE DISTRACTIONS on a fresh sheet of paper.

Baxter glanced over and tapped the paper. "So, which distraction are you going to use? Pretending to eat off the ground? Faking a broken arm, like a bird?"

"No. None of those." Waylon tugged his hair, thinking hard.

Marco dropped down next to Waylon then. "Food is a great distraction," he said. "But don't eat off the ground."

Maria poked her head in between them. "I'm good at faking stuff. I could fake a broken arm, no problem."

Waylon ignored Marco and Maria, too.

Just then, Baxter's padlock sprang open with a joyful snap. "Yes!" he and Waylon cried at the same time, and then fist-bumped each other. And as Waylon's knuckles knocked Baxter's, it occurred to him: just a few days earlier, he'd been worried that Arlo Brody might see him with Baxter.

It seemed so long ago. A dog's life ago. It seemed ridiculous now.

He looked over to the Shark-Punchers' headquarters. There stood Arlo, watching. Alone. Waylon had never seen him alone before. Waylon's hand rose, although he hadn't told it to. It waved to Arlo. Arlo smiled and started over.

Waylon looked at his hand. He didn't know why it had waved. Alien Hand Syndrome—he might actually have it. But right now, Waylon couldn't even get excited about this possibility—he and Baxter were planning a life-or-death escape plot, and it was hard to care about anything else.

Baxter nudged Waylon then. "Remember,

172

this is a police station. Cops have seen every-thing. You need to bust some kind of flashy moves to distract these people."

Arlo crouched down in front of them. "What people?" he asked. "Why do you want to dis-tract them?"

Waylon didn't answer. There would proba-bly be a price to pay for ignoring Arlo—King Arlo had probably never been ignored before—but Waylon didn't care about that, either.

Because suddenly he could see Dumpster Eddy's face as though it was right in front of him. Eddy's brown eyes were begging for free-dom. "Don't worry," Waylon vowed to Baxter. "I'll figure something out."

"Something *epic*," Baxter said.

"Epic," Waylon agreed. "You just handle the getaway."

For the next ten minutes, he and Baxter

plotted timelines, finished maps, and brain-stormed strategy while the other kids watched.

"The distraction has to be something really wild," Baxter urged.

Waylon tugged up more tufts. Recess was almost over. And then he grinned. "Or not!" He scribbled LIVING STATUE under EPIC STRATEGY.

"Living statue?" Baxter asked. *"Living statue?"*

Just then the bell rang. Waylon and Baxter scrambled to their feet. Waylon threw his arm around Baxter's shoulders. "Trust me," he said. "It's going to be awesome!"

"There's a bus stop a block east of the police station," Baxter called as they ran to line up. "We meet there at ten fifteen tomorrow."

16

Waylon got to the bus stop early. He pulled on the Ben Franklin costume and cinched it as tight he could. "How do I look?" he asked when Baxter showed up.

Baxter studied him for a minute. "Like Ben Franklin's kid dressing up in his father's clothes," he said at last.

"Fine." Waylon took a marker and added JR. to the BEN FRANKLIN sign on the box, then handed Baxter the marble-gray makeup.

When his face and hands were painted, he

put on the spectacles. Waylon was happy to find that his dad had only smeared them thinly with paint. They looked like stone from the outside, but he could see through them perfectly well.

Just then, a car pulled up to the curb. Marco got out, carrying a big tray. "Wow, you look really . . . gray," he told Waylon.

"Good," Waylon said. "What are you doing here?"

Marco lifted the edge of the tin foil. "Tamales. Food is a great distraction."

"Distraction? You're going to help us?" Baxter asked.

Waylon leaned over and sniffed. He was distracted already. Before he could thank Marco, Rasheed and Charlie appeared on their skateboards.

Rasheed wore a sign around his neck that read HUMAN CALCULATOR—TEST ME!

"I've memorized ninety-six knock-knock jokes," Charlie said. "That'll keep someone occupied for at least fifteen minutes."

Maria skidded up on her bike next. She grabbed her arm and groaned. "The hurt wing fake-out," she explained. "If it's good enough for birds, it's good enough for me."

And then around the corner came Buddy, dragging Joe by the leash. "If there's any get-away barking," Joe promised when he caught his breath, "Buddy will take the fall."

"Thanks," Waylon said. "And, hey . . . you look taller."

"My dad burned waffles this morning." Joe beamed and pointed to his shoes. "They're a little scratchy, but they're giving me half an inch."

The police staff was pretty surprised that a bunch of kids had taken them up on their offer to visit any time. Except the dispatcher. She just sat at her desk looking bored.

While the other kids spread out over the lobby, Baxter positioned himself near the padlocked door. Waylon dropped his box directly opposite.

Just then, the lobby doors opened and Arlo Brody came racing in, carrying a soccer ball. He ran over to Waylon. "I can dribble continuously while reciting all fifty state capitals. Would that be okay?"

For a moment, Waylon was speechless. Arlo Brody was looking at him as if it would be an incredible honor to do this thing for him. "That would be cool," Waylon finally answered. "Thanks, Arlo." And then he climbed onto his

marble gray–painted box and struck his pose.

It turned out Baxter was wrong about the police—you really didn't have to put on much of a show to get their attention. Which made sense when Waylon thought about it—and standing perfectly still on his box gave him plenty of time to think about it. If your normal police station is full of robbers and drunks and people acting crazy because of the full moon, why wouldn't eight kids doing regular things seem pretty bizarre?

In just a few minutes, the lobby was filled with blue uniforms visiting the distractions. Police officers swiped tamale after tamale off Marco's tray as if they hadn't had a decent meal in weeks, they laughed at Charlie's knock-knock jokes, and they wandered around Waylon, admiring him doing nothing.

Two officers assured Maria her arm was

fine but wrapped it in a sling anyway. For good measure, they bandaged her head and took her blood pressure.

The police chief challenged Rasheed to a multiplication duel and lost every round. "Gambling is illegal, son," he reminded Rasheed. "Otherwise, you'd have made a fortune."

Only Arlo Brody stood alone. As a distraction display, he turned out to be kind of a dud. But whenever he smiled, a predictable thing happened: the police officers smiled back as though they had been hypnotized. And that, Waylon had to admit, couldn't hurt.

Unfortunately, though, none of the distractions distracted the one person who needed to be distracted. The dispatcher kept working at her desk, only flicking her eyes over the scene from time to time.

What would it take to catch her attention?

Waylon's legs started to tremble. But every time he thought about breaking his pose, he remembered grokking with Dumpster Eddy, and he locked his knees solidly in place again.

Through the paint-smeared spectacles, Waylon saw Baxter take the tiniest step backward. And then he remembered: the trick to being a living statue wasn't holding still, it was moving! The next time the dispatcher flicked her eyes over him, Waylon twitched his nose.

She startled. She shook her head.

Waylon held perfectly still as she studied him, then he dipped a quick bow.

The dispatcher raised her eyebrows. Then she locked her drawer, got up, and perched on the side of her desk. With her back to the big steel door.

Baxter dropped to his knees at the lock.

Waylon held steady another full minute. Then he tipped his head and winked at the dispatcher over his glasses, his father's best trick.

The dispatcher threw back her head and laughed.

And when Waylon checked again, Baxter was gone!

Five minutes to set Eddy free and another ten for him to get safely away—that was the plan. Fifteen more minutes of holding still was a long time.

The trick is to go inside yourself, his father often said. Waylon hadn't understood before, but now he did. He set his gaze on the ceiling and went so deep inside himself that there in the middle of the crowded police station lobby, he heard his living sounds again.

As before, every once in a while there was a little skip. This time, though, Waylon was thankful he wasn't teleporting anywhere. Because there was no place in the universe he would rather be than right here, playing a part in Operation Free Eddy, with so many of his friends around him.

And then, from the corner of his eye, he caught a brown streak flashing past the lobby doors. Waylon kept his face perfectly rigid, but inside, he grinned and whooped. The streak had zoomed by too quickly for him to have identified it, and yet somehow he had: a scruffy little dog with a lopsided grin, his ears flapping free in the wind, his stick-skinny legs just a blur.

Waylon relocked his muscles. The last ten minutes were the hardest, his father always said. *Your stomach does you in—you're always starving the last ten minutes.* And sure enough, his stomach was suddenly a hollow crater.

Rosie's Bakery was a block away, but he could swear he smelled cupcakes—chocolate with marshmallow frosting, three dollars each. Minute after agonizing minute, his legs ached and his mouth watered.

Just when he couldn't take it a second longer,

Baxter Boylen sauntered in through the front doors and flashed victory fingers.

Waylon jumped down from the box, the other kids dropped what they were doing, and the entire police staff erupted in applause.

It took a while to get out, because the police officers all wanted to say "Thanks for stopping by," and "Don't forget to stay safe." When Waylon finally gathered up his stuff, he was surprised to see that his hat was stuffed with tips. Twenty-four dollars and thirty-five cents!

Waylon led the kids down the street.

"Eight, please," he told Rosie, handing her all the bills. "Chocolate with marshmallow frosting."

As he dropped the change into the tip jar, he heard a scratching at the window.

Galaxy. Waylon recognized the hungry look on his face—Waylon had drooled at this same window with those same sad eyes the past seven weeks. Chocolate wasn't good for dogs, but Rosie's had plenty of non-chocolate things, too. He dug in his pockets. Nothing.

And Rosie read his mind.

She lifted a giant peanut-butter cookie from the case, bent down, and dropped it gently onto the floor. "What a shame," she said, picking it up. "Now I can't sell it." She put it in a bag and handed it to Waylon with a wink.

Outside, Waylon led the way across the street to the park.

Galaxy gulped his cookie in a single bite. Everyone else sprawled on the grass, licking frosting slowly and reliving the rescue.

"We were so cool," Arlo said. "Hey, I know!
We should form a team!"

Waylon shot Arlo a glare—not as sizzling as

Neon's, but plenty hot. So did Baxter and Joe and Charlie and Rasheed and Maria and Marco.

Arlo threw up his hands. "All on one team. I meant to say that!"

Baxter leaned back on his elbows. "Eddy took off like a shot. I wish I knew where he went."

"I saw a dog hanging out at the ice cream stand this summer," Charlie said. "He followed the littlest kids around, lapping up their spills. Maybe Eddy's there."

Rasheed pointed to the pond. "I hope he's chasing ducks. Ducks honk when you chase them."

"Or napping in the sun," Joe said. "Buddy loves to nap in the sun."

Buddy cocked his head at his name. He stretched and then settled down in front of Waylon. Waylon scratched his neck while the others went on imagining the things Eddy might be doing.

Waylon liked picturing them all. But when he closed his eyes he saw something else. He saw Dumpster Eddy running, his ears flapping free in the wind and his stick-skinny legs just a blur.

After dinner, Waylon sat on his bed with his journal. Maybe Operation Free Eddy wasn't a scientific achievement, but it was part of his life's work. It deserved to be recorded for history.

As he closed the cover, he heard a knock.

"Play OAT," Neon said from the doorway.

Waylon crossed his arms and lay back. There

had been a lot of awesome things in the day. But one, of course, was best. "Dumpster Eddy is free."

"And you and this Baxter—are you friends now?"

"I don't know. We're not not-friends anyway. Actually, the whole class is not not-friends again now."

"Because of today?" Neon asked. "That's great."

"Mostly because pinecone sap ruins clothes. Everybody's parents were really mad about the team thing on Wednesday night. But yep, also because of today."

"A single day with a friend is more valuable than a lifetime with a bar of gold."

Waylon looked at his sister, surprised. Did she remember that was a line from *Lonelyville*? *"You can't cry on the shoulder of a bar of gold,"* he answered, watching her carefully.

"Or eat popcorn at midnight with it," Neon answered with a grin. Then she tipped her head toward the living room.

"Are you sure?" Waylon asked.

She held up a comb. "Hurry up. Before I change my mind."

Waylon scrambled off the bed.

In the living room, Neon plunked down at her mother's knees and handed her the comb. Mrs. Zakowski kissed the top of her head and began braiding.

"Trust is the timber that built the house of our friendship, Louise Pembleton. Yours has rotted away!" Waylon quoted, plopping onto the couch next to his mom.

"Punish me if you must, but don't turn your backs on me!" Neon answered, her hand flung dramatically to her brow.

Mr. Zakowski stared for a moment. Then he

flew off the couch, knelt in front of his daughter, and hugged her so hard, Waylon thought she'd be crushed.

Neon struggled out of his hug enough to moan, *"Don't send me to Lonelyville!"* and everybody broke into the kind of laughter that usually made Mrs. Zakowski remind them their furniture wasn't waterproof. Which she didn't do this time because she was laughing too hard.

And just then the strange, seeing-himself-from-the-outside thing happened again. The boy Waylon saw had brought his family back together. Somehow, he had managed to connect Baxter and the other kids, too. *Isthmus* was a hard thing to say and a dumb thing to blurt out in a classroom. But it was a fine thing to be.

THE END
(almost)

Monday morning, Baxter Boylen came to school with a face that looked like the whole world had sat on it.

"They picked him up again last night," he moaned. "In a Dumpster behind China Delight. He jumped right into the squad car with a sparerib still in his mouth."

Baxter collapsed onto his desk and buried his head in his hands. But Waylon felt strangely elated at the news. When he stood up, he felt as if he were floating.

As if gravity had loosened its grip.

He put a hand on Baxter's shoulder. "No, it's going to be fine. Because we have ten whole days this time," he said. "It's going to be *even more awesome!*"

THE END